This charming menagerie of friends shows readers that knowledge often comes from the most unlikely places.

"Gomi's meticulous sense of design and careful use of brilliantly colored, highly delineated images imbues the story with a sense of the wonder and delight to be derived from life's simplest—but bountiful—moments."
—*Publishers Weekly*

"A little girl recites all the pleasurable things she has learned from her friends . . . including such meaningful things as reading and studying and, most importantly, loving . . . An elemental story that will reach toddlers and older preschoolers alike."
—*Booklist*

"Taro Gomi has once more created a perfect blend of art and text in this simple picture book in which a little girl's animal friends demonstrate some basic actions learned in life . . . The straightforward text is rhythmic, and the graphic collage style is brilliantly colored."
—*The Five Owls*

"The illustrations are vibrant. The story is simple . . . Children will quickly be pointing out the whimsical details in the art."
—*Parents' Choice*

First published in the United States in hardcover in 1990 by Chronicle Books LLC. Copyright © 1989 by Taro Gomi. English text copyright © 1990 by Chronicle Books LLC. All rights reserved. First published in Japan by Ehonkan Publishers, Tokyo. English translation rights arranged through Japan Foreign rights Centre. Manufactured in China.

ISBN 0-8118-1237-5 (pbk.)

Library of Congress Cataloging-in-Publication Data

Gomi, Taro.
   [Minna ga oshiete kuremashita. English]
   My friends / by Taro Gomi
      p.cm.
   Translation of: Minna ga oshiete kuremashita.
   Summary: A little girl learns to walk, climb, and study the earth from her friends, most of whom are animals.
   [1. Growth – Fiction. 2. Animals – Fiction.] I. Title.
   PZ7.GS586My   1990   [E] – dc20   89-239040
                                                                   CIP
                                                                   AC

Distributed in Canada by Raincoast Books, 9050 Shaughnessy Street, Vancouver, British Columbia V6P 6E5

10 9 8

Chronicle Books LLC, 85 Second Street, San Francisco, California 94105

www.chroniclekids.com

MY FRIENDS

by Taro Gomi

chronicle books

www.chroniclekids.com

I learned to walk from my friend
the cat.

I learned to jump from my friend the dog.

I learned to climb from my friend
the monkey.

I learned to run from my friend
the horse.

I learned to march from my friend
the rooster.

I learned to nap from

my friend the crocodile.

I learned to smell the flowers
from my friend the butterfly.

I learned to hide from

my friend the rabbit.

I learned to explore the earth from

my friend the ant.

I learned to kick from my friend
the gorilla.

I learned to watch the night sky
from my friend the owl.

I learned to sing from my friends the birds.

I learned to read from

my friends the books.

I learned to study from

my friends the teachers.

I learned to play from

my friends at school.

And I learned to love from a friend like you.

TARO GOMI attended the Kuwazawa Design School in Tokyo. He has illustrated more than one hundred books for children, garnering him many awards. Mr. Gomi now lives in Tokyo, Japan.

OTHER TARO GOMI BOOKS AVAILABLE FROM CHRONICLE BOOKS

Spring Is Here
Bus Stops